CLICK FOR CHAOS

LAYLA NOX

CONTENTS

CONTENT WARNINGS

Click for Chaos is a cozy mystery, but it wouldn't be me if it wasn't at least a little bit dark. This story deals with themes of poverty, corruption, and revenge. Please put your mental health first.

- Capitalist corruption
- Death of a parent (off page)
- Mild violence
- Depression
- Poverty
- Prejudice
- Revenge
- Some explicit language

For the ones who struggle every day - against the system, society, and even ourselves.

CLICK FOR CHAOS

LAYLA NOX

The hardest part about walking to work was resisting all the distractions of Stratos.

Chatter hung in the city's air like smog, individual conversations blending together into a chorus of liveliness. A delicious smell wafted past from a pretzel stand, making Opal's mouth water. Flower boxes drew her gaze with their vibrant colors and fragrant blooms.

Two years ago, Opal moved to the city to get a tiny bit of freedom from the suffocating affection of her family. She loved them all dearly, but they were overbearing and overstimulating at best.

She still visited most weekends for family dinner, opting to use a portal due to her lack of a vehicle. She came from a long line of witches, and most of them had a mild amount of magic. Enough to get by and make life a little easier, but nothing life-changing. They were always pleased to see her, begging for news from the big city and her fancy job.

Her job was, in fact, *not* fancy, but they wouldn't hear anything about that. They were *very* proud. She managed to land a job at the help desk of a tech conglomerate called Dreamedia shortly after she moved, and spent the last two years clinging to it for dear life.

Really, all she did was chat with customers, ask them to turn their machines off and back on, and then escalate their issue to the real tech support team if that didn't work. It was a pretty cushy job, and the pay wasn't bad either. She even scored an afternoon shift, so she got to spend her mornings leisurely tending to the tiny garden on her balcony and enjoying coffee with the birds.

Her apartment was a few blocks away, and the walk to work every morning was one of her favorite things. The sun shone bright between the skyscrapers of the city, warming her face and refracting rainbows in the towering glass windows.

It was lunchtime for most, and the food carts were out in full swing. Opal waved to all the vendors, and they returned her waves with warm smiles. She stopped at their carts on her way to work whenever she could afford it. Unfortunately, today was not one of those days, and there was a peanut butter and elderberry jelly sandwich in her backpack for later.

As Opal stepped into the glass spinning doors of Dreamedia's lobby, a hulking orc in a tailored suit sped in from the other side. His momentum spun the doors far too fast, and she was nearly knocked over from the force. She stumbled out on the other side, barely keeping herself from falling face first on the marble tile.

She whipped around, catching a glimpse of the orc before he got too far. She recognized him as one of the territory sales agents who worked the early morning shift, probably leaving for the day.

"Better hurry up," she grumbled under her breath. "Wouldn't want to be late for *home,* asshole." She rolled her eyes and let the annoyance fade before stepping up to the lobby desk.

"Hey, Larisa!" Opal called cheerily to the receptionist. "Anything fun happen this morning?"

"Hey, girl! Nothing really," the water nymph replied, tossing her voluminous deep blue hair over her shoulder. Her flawless skin had a faint blue tint, and she wore a mesh corset under her black blazer. "I'm out of here in an hour, though. There's still time."

Both women laughed, waving each other off before Opal headed through the big doors next to the desk. They lead to a wall of elevators, each with their own attendant. The elevator in front of the door was available, which *never* happened, and Opal took it as a good omen for the day.

"Good afternoon, Mr. Dieg," she said, stepping in next to the brownie attendant on his stool. He grinned at her and bowed his tiny head, pressing the button for the thirty-seventh floor. He was a sweet little fae, and he was always polite to her, but he never spoke. She only knew his name from the name tag on his tiny red uniform.

When the elevator hit her floor and the door started to open, Dieg tapped Opal's arm with his closed fist. She smiled, holding out her open palm, and Dieg dropped a peppermint candy into it. Opal thanked him and he gave her another bow. She made a mental note to bring him a bit of milk tomorrow as a thank you.

As she stepped through the doors, she cast a quick sparkler charm behind her, raining down a tiny light show of rainbow sparkles in the elevator that would dissolve into the air before they hit the ground. Dieg's delighted squeals echoed as the doors closed, and Opal grinned to herself. That would do for today.

She made her way down the quiet hall to her department, pushing open the door to a cacophony of chaos. This was one of twelve help desk stations in the monstrous building, with an average of thirty agents working in each one at any given time. Most of them made little effort to keep the noise down, so it was always a little excessive. Opal had grown used to it by now, the discordant yapping a comforting presence rather than a grating distraction.

She hurried over to her desk, settling in for her shift with a practiced ease. She slid her headset on, the band resting against the giant knot of violet hair that was perched precariously on top of her head.

A snap of her finger lit the salted caramel candle next to her monitor. Another snap flipped the switch that turned on the small lamp on the other side and started up her computer.

Little magics like these and Dieg's little light show were the majority of Opal's powers. Parlor tricks and petty magics were enough to continue calling herself a witch, but she'd never been able to make a living out of it. Which is why she ended up at Dreamedia.

As her system came to life, she quickly clocked in and waited for her first call of the day.

———

EVENING TRAFFIC WAS the worst part of the day. Quinn weaved in and out of the gridlocked cars on Fifth Ave, ignoring the honking horns. The air was choked with smog and the light pollution concealed all of the stars. Even with a UV blocking helmet, the fading light of sunset was enough to irritate his eyes.

He hopped his bike up onto the sidewalk and cut through an alley, dodging dumpsters and the stray trash littered around them. The smell was putrid, creeping up into his helmet and invading his preternaturally sensitive nose. He sped up, eager to get out of the cesspool.

Back out on the road, he revved his bike and rushed through the last block to the parking garage. As soon as he was underground, the strain on his eyes lessened. The cold air and industrial smell of the concrete lot was a significant improvement from the pollen-infested, plebeian wasteland of the city in springtime.

The only people who parked in the enclosed garage were the other nocturnally inclined employees, which were, luckily, few and far between. Quinn pulled into a spot and slid off his helmet, pushing his dark hair straight back until it curled below his ears. With his helmet tucked under his arm, he made his way to the elevators.

"Basement three," he grumbled, and the brownie in the elevator eyed him warily from his stool before pressing the button labeled 'B3'. Quinn had worked at Dreamedia for nine years now, and he still had to tell the little bastards what floor he worked on. It would be infinitely less irritating if they didn't look at him like he was about to eat them the entire ride down.

Quinn was what they called a vegan vampire, much to the dismay of his family. Like all vampires, he lived on blood. Humanoid creatures provided the most sustenance and the longest time between feeding, but the thought of consuming something that came out of someone living in *this* city was repulsive, so he sustained himself strictly on bottles of synthetic blood from the bodega.

Brownies were very much *not* on the menu.

The elevator dinged, the doors sliding open slowly, and Quinn rushed out, eager to remove himself from the awkward silence. He headed down the hall and retreated to the privacy of his office next to the server room, hanging his helmet on the rounded hook next to the door.

The equipment they provided him with when he first started was mediocre at best, so he personally refurnished the entire office out of his own admittedly deep pockets. Might as well put that family money to good use, right?

Quinn was the tenth heir to the Devane family fortune, which meant... Well, not much. Despite looking to be in his mid-twenties thanks to his genetically halted aging, he was the second youngest of his siblings at thirty-six. Most of them were hundreds of years old, and the eldest were all squarely positioned in the family business.

His parents were exactly what one would expect from a centuries-old power couple. Simultaneously hands-off and entirely too involved, but at all the wrong times. They desperately wanted all of their children to follow in their footsteps, spending their hoarded wealth and infinite years on the best business and law schools and eventually joining the family law firm.

When Quinn expressed a desire to delve into the digital world, they weren't mad. They were just *disappointed*, which was always worse somehow. They supported his decision, though, paying for his schooling and lifestyle despite clearly hoping that he would eventually get bored with ones and zeroes and come to his senses.

He did not.

Over a decade later, he had carved out a nice position for himself as Head of Cybersecurity at Dreamedia. It came with a nice paycheck and plenty of perks, although he still had access to his family's absurd fortune for fun upgrades like the top-of-the-line PC setup that lay before him.

As his computer booted up, he grabbed a bottle of Pulse from the mini-fridge next to his desk and stuck it in the microwave before settling in. He rarely had visitors in his office, but the wall of monitors provided an additional barrier from the general population just in case.

Every day started with sorting through dozens of emails about escalated tickets, potential security issues, and various other future trash bin items. The customer service reps at Dreamedia seemed to think that every little operator error needed to be escalated.

Plot twist. They definitely did *not*.

Honestly, it was like they didn't have any faith in his technical prowess. As if anyone could get through his firewalls. It might be laughable if it weren't so damn frustrating.

The first email in his inbox was escalated by a rep named Opal Noakes. He didn't make a habit of mingling with the revolving door of employees at Dreamedia, but Opal was a frequent flyer in his inbox. Quinn glanced at the email's subject with a scowl.

Ticket 749385 Escalation – Security Breach

Security breach, my undead ass, he thought. There wasn't a snow sprite's chance in hell that someone breached his security. With a sigh, he opened the email and got to work.

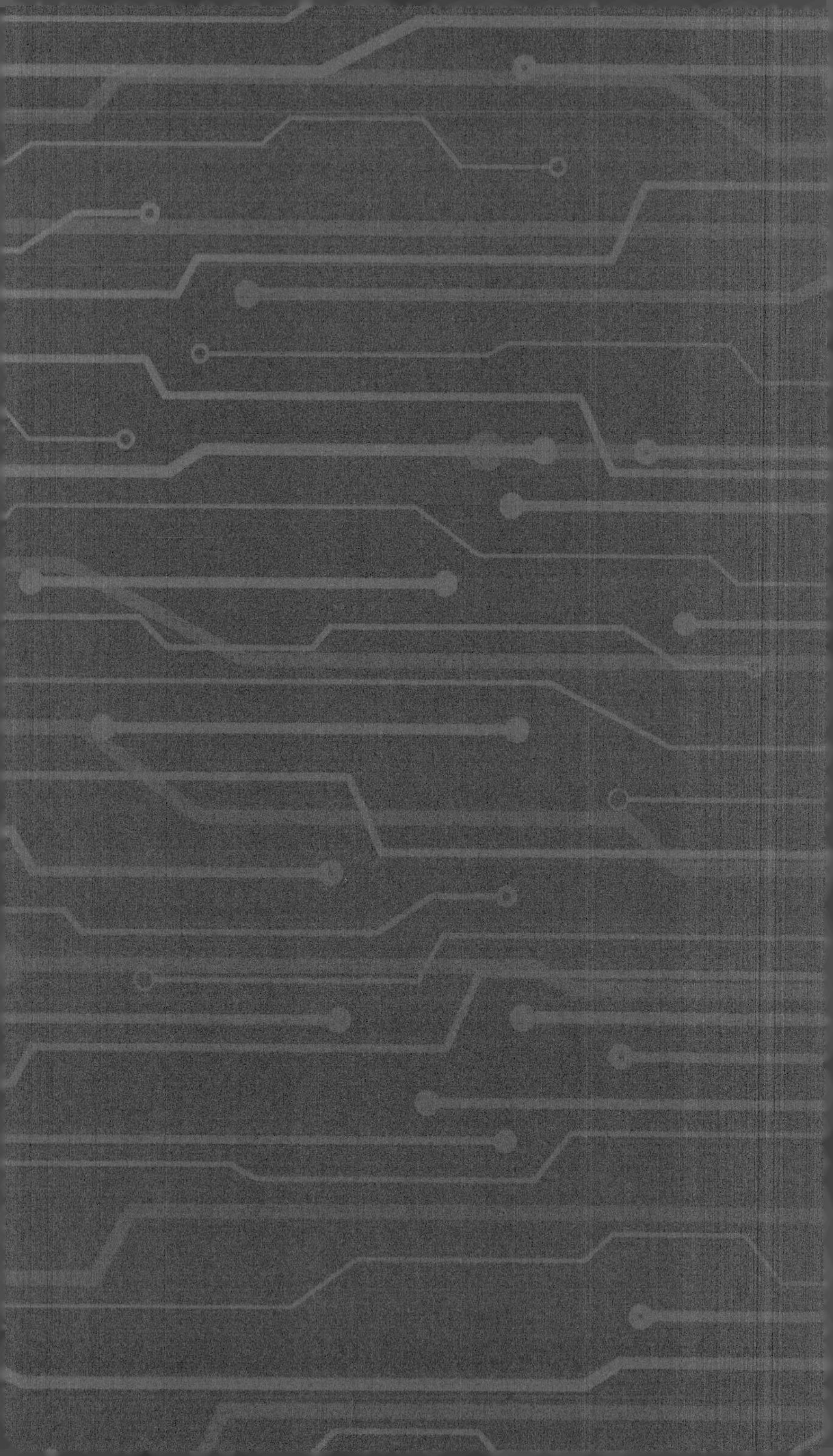

"Dreamedia Customer Service, this is Opal. How can I provide the service of your dreams today?" Opal regurgitated with an excess of fake cheer.

She still cringed every time she had to greet a caller with the cheesy company line. Dreamedia manufactured and sold various products that ran on the energy produced by dreaming, and their marketing leaned heavily into the dream puns. It was one of the main reasons that she preferred dealing with help desk tickets over calls.

"Yeah, hi," the flustered woman on the other end mumbled. "My name is Maria and.. Um, well, I guess I'm not sure what happened. I've got one of the new recording devices with the hologram projection. I don't remember the model. Anyway, I'm an oneiric seer, and I use it to project my dreams for my customers. I had a nightmare a few days ago that I was mugged, and it was recorded, but it wasn't prophetic or anything. Just a nightmare. Well... it happened. Today."

"Oh, no! I'm sorry that happened to you," Opal said sincerely. Most of her coworkers were apathetic toward customers, placating them just enough to get through the call and on to the next, but Opal genuinely cared about them. Probably a little too much. "That must have been very stressful. I hope you weren't hurt!"

"No, I'm okay," Maria assured her. "It was a few hours ago, and they just pushed me down a bit. They *did* steal my purse, though. Not much you can do about that part, I suppose. But I wanted to call and report it because there must be a data breach somewhere. There's just no way that I dreamt something that specific and it happened exactly the same way just a few days later. Trust me, I know a prophetic dream when I see one, and this was definitely not one."

"That *is* peculiar," Opal agreed, putting on her best customer service voice. "Is it possible that it was a coincidence? What happened, exactly?"

"No, I don't think so. I was attacked on the street in broad daylight by someone in a mask!" Opal let out a small gasp that egged her on. "It was a specific mask, too. It was one of those blank face ones with little designs painted on it. I'm sure I saw it somewhere in my travels before, but it's not the sort of thing that someone would use in a mugging."

"Well, let me get your information so we can look up your model. " After Maria provided some account details, Opal confirmed her device was showing as operational with no errors or security breaches. She didn't want to brush off her concerns, though, so she started opening a ticket.

"Alright, Maria. I've got your ticket created and I'll escalate all of this to the senior cybersecurity team to review. Again, I'm so sorry that you're going through all of this. Hopefully things will look up for you soon!"

Opal rattled off a ticket number and Maria thanked her for everything before hanging up. Once everything was in the system, she put all the details in an email to the cybersecurity team, as promised.

She was positive that the other teams in the building hated to see her coming, both in person and in their inboxes. She was, admittedly, a bit of an over-escalator, but she'd rather be safe than sorry.

As soon as she hit send, her phone rang. She took a deep breath and dove back into her customer service voice.

"Dreamedia Customer Service, this is Opal!"

———

A FEW HOURS LATER, Opal was running out of steam. It seemed like every single call was from someone with a major issue and a matching attitude. It was nearly time to go, and she was watching the clock like she could will it to move faster.

The next caller was finally a polite customer, but Opal could tell from the moment he started talking that this was going to be a nightmare.

"Well, I'm not exactly sure, but I think someone hacked into my DreamBank," the man's gruff voice explained. The DreamBank was an outdated Dreamedia product that harnessed the astral kinetic energy created by dreams and used it to provide power to a portable battery bank. It was popular among the blue collar working class for its affordability and convenience while out on jobs, but it was unfortunately famous for spontaneous combustion.

"Oh, boy," Opal said. "Why do you think that?

"I, uh... I'm on the construction crew for that new apartment building that's going up over on North Fable. I had a nightmare the other day that one of the ceiling beams fell and crushed me. It was funny because I'm carrying those things around all day, so there's no way one of them falling on me could do any real damage. But, in the dream, the beam was massive. Or maybe I was small? I don't remember."

"Dreams are funny like that," Opal chimed in.

"Exactly," he agreed. "Anyway, I was on the job site today and when I looked up, there was a huge beam about to fall on me. It had to be enchanted, because it was bigger than the whole apartment building. My buddy saw it before I did and pulled me out of the way just in time, but, when it hit the ground, it exploded into some sticky glitter. The whole crew is covered in it, and it doesn't wash off."

"That is definitely bizarre," Opal mused. "Sounds like someone conjured up an illudo irrito spell. Did you tell anyone about the dream when it happened?"

"No, ma'am. That felt a little like asking for some bad luck, to be honest. I didn't tell a soul," he swore.

"Does anyone else have access to your account?" she asked. "Anyone who might have downloaded the data themselves?"

"Not that I know of. My brother lives with me, but he wouldn't have my login or anything."

"Hmm. Okay, what about any sketchy connections? Did you use your DreamBank on any public networks at a job site or anything? Maybe connected to a neighbor's wifi?"

"Nah, I don't connect it to anything but my home internet. My brother and I live over on Walnut Road in Little Benevento, so the neighbors are mostly low-tech witches and their home apothecaries. Not really the hacker crowd."

She was about to remind him that he was currently talking to a witch about tech support, but her gaze snagged on the tiny clock on her screen and she decided it was time to wrap up this episode of CSI. She could do some more investigation after the professionals took a look.

"Hmm, okay. Well, Mr. Zugarod, I'm going to get a ticket submitted for this, and I promise I'll escalate it to the higher ups!"

That seemed to satisfy him. He thanked her for her help before hanging up, and she paused her call queue so she could type out all the details before submitting the escalation request.

At the very beginning of the report, she added in all caps, "SECOND TIME TODAY – PLEASE INVESTIGATE". Hopefully that would get someone's attention.

———

WITH THE HEAVIEST sigh he could muster, Quinn clicked on the newest email in his inbox.

"Shocker," he muttered under his breath. "Opal Noakes escalated a ticket." He rolled his eyes, cursor poised and ready over the trash bin icon. This was her seventh escalated ticket today, and only one of them was remotely suspicious. It was, unfortunately, an improvement from yesterday's *twelve* escalations.

The witch simply did not know the meaning of the word "important".

The ticket for the possible threat from earlier had ultimately proved to be nothing, and Quinn's team had chalked it up to operator error before it had even gotten to him to make the final call. The customer obviously had her device connected to the city-wide wifi or some other shared network, and someone hacked into it and downloaded her local files.

Quinn raised an eyebrow at the screen, squinting at the big, bold letters slapped across the top of the email. *Second time today, huh?*

After reading the details, he sighed again. DreamBanks were famous for their many faults, and one of them was being incredibly susceptible to hackers. The tiniest bit of technical know-how could wreak havoc on a DreamBank. So, yet again, this was probably a case of operator error.

Quinn pulled up the device by the serial number in the ticket and ran a few log reports on it. He expected to find a handful of malicious attacks within a short time, followed by one small breach, a download of data, and then back to business as usual. What he found, though, was unexpected.

A singular, targeted breach followed by a small download of data. From an IP address that lead back to Dreamedia HQ.

Well, shit.

He dug a little deeper, desperate to find some evidence that this breach didn't come from his own team, or from within his own firewalls. There was just no way that it could have come from outside. No one could have gotten through his security.

He spent the rest of his shift digging, and not a single report showed any additional information. Nothing to support any kind of actual breach. Once he was satisfied that there was nothing else to find, he closed the ticket and left.

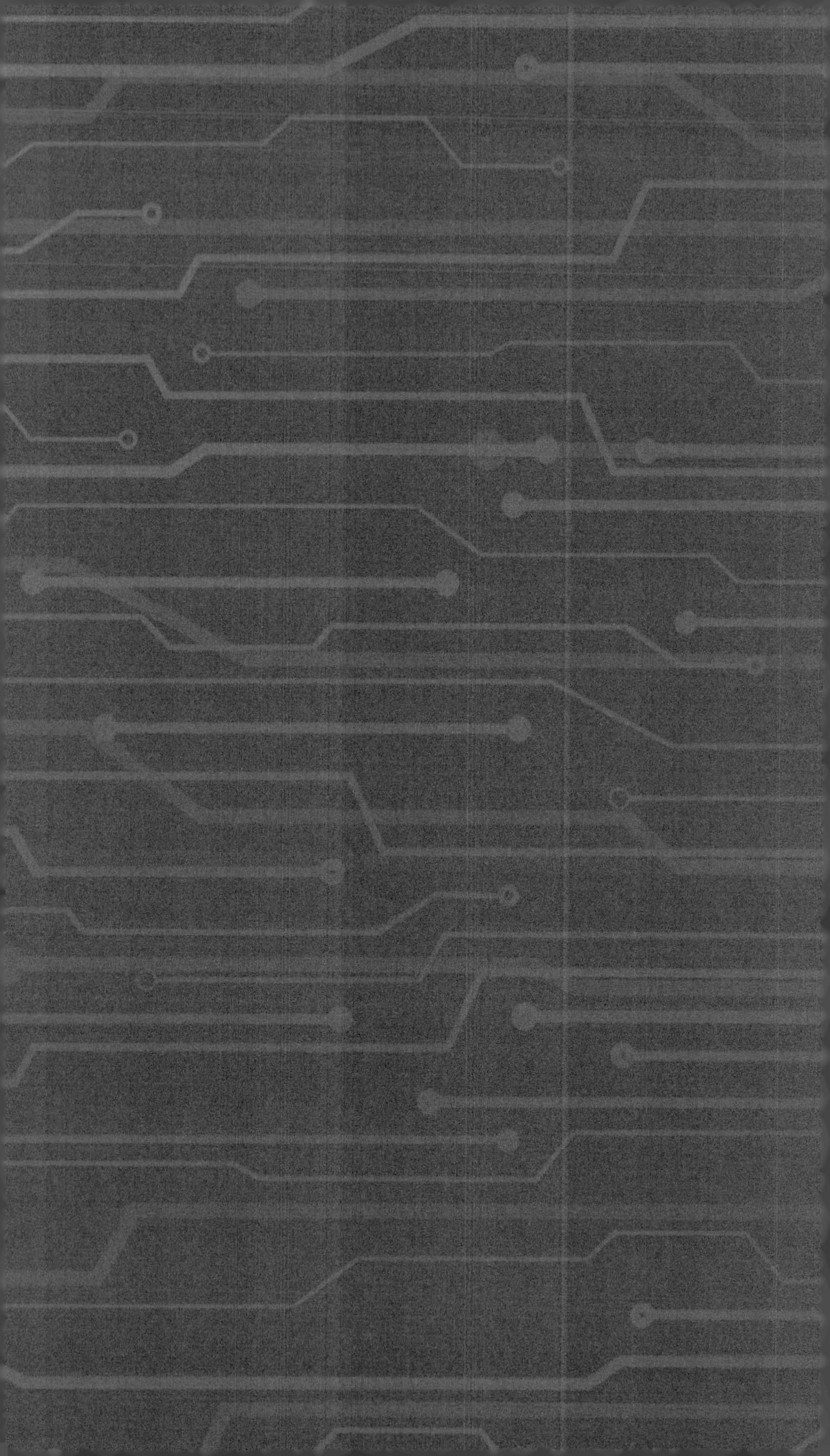

The next day, Opal made sure to check on her tickets as soon as she got in. She was infuriated to see that they had *all* been closed with no further action required. She usually anticipated her escalated tickets to be closed. She often didn't even bother following up with them.

But she couldn't shake the feeling that something was amiss.

She opened the ticket logs and saw that it was none other than the Undead Stormcloud himself, Quinn Devane, who had closed both of the security breach tickets. He was famously rude and uninviting, known for his unbelievably condescending demeanor and sky-high opinion of himself and literally no one else.

It was mostly just hearsay, though, because no one but his cybersecurity team ever actually interacted with him.

Granted, he was a cybersecurity prodigy. Or so she had heard, anyway. He had singlehandedly built the entire security system of Dreamedia, inside and out, from the ground up.

But that didn't mean he could be a dick about it.

Opal decided she would have to take things into her own hands and make a personal appearance down in the server room. She had never actually met Quinn in person, but today was apparently the day. Due to his nocturnal nature, he wouldn't be in the office for another few hours.

So she would sit and wait. And she would *stew*.

There were only a few windows in Opal's office, but she doubted she would see him driving in anyway. Surely, he and his flashy motorcycle were too good for the public entrance. She figured he would be in around sundown. As soon as the sun set, she paused her call queue and headed downstairs with the ticket numbers in hand.

She took the stairs to calm her nerves, but it didn't have the intended effect. She was clenching her sticky note so tight that her fingers were shaking. She made her way past the server room and held up a hand to the door, hesitating just below the golden plaque with his stupid name on it.

With a deep breath, she rapped on the door twice.

"Come in," came an annoyed voice from inside, followed by some unintelligible mumbling.

Opal opened the door and stepped inside, ready to greet him with a reluctant smile, only to be met with a wall of monitors. A mess of dark, curly hair was barely visible in the gaps, but he made no attempt to acknowledge her. *Typical.*

"Hi, I'm Opal!" she said, stepping around the monitors so she could see him. He might be good looking if his face hadn't been scrunched up in annoyance. His high cheekbones and plush lips were marred by a scowl that would hurl daggers if it could.

"Yes, I assumed," he sighed, as if her mere presence was tedious. "What can I help you with, Opal?"

"Well," she started, holding the sticky note out for him. He stared at it like it was poisonous for a moment before taking it from her. "I noticed that these tickets were closed yesterday with no action taken."

He blinked at her and said nothing. The *'and…?'* was clearly implied.

"I want to know why nothing was done," she continued, mustering up her best assertive voice. Opal *hated* confrontation. She could already feel the heat creeping up her neck, and her face was starting to feel itchy. "There was clearly an issue."

Quinn took a deep, condescending breath before he answered her. It took every ounce of Opal's self control not to roll her eyes. She was pretty sure he didn't even need to *breathe*, let alone take one that big.

"Well, Opal," he said, with a tone meant for a toddler. "I'm not sure why you're under the impression that nothing was done. I personally looked into both cases, ran multiple reports, and determined that, while admittedly abnormal, both cases were simply operator error. There was no evidence that anything else needed to be done."

"I... But, there was nothing in the notes about that," Opal sputtered. "The files both just said *ticket closed by Quinn Devane.*"

"My time is limited, Opal. I'm not in the habit of explaining my efforts on tickets that would presumably stay closed once I've closed them." He raised an accusatory brow at her, and she glared in return. The absolute *nerve* of this guy.

"Well, maybe you should start. Us *peons* like to make sure that the promises we're making to customers are actually being fulfilled and not just swept under the rug." He actually rolled his eyes at her, mumbling something presumably infuriating. She couldn't hear him over the blood rushing in her ears.

"Yes, well," he said, waving a dismissive hand at her. "Now you know. So if there's nothing else..." His gaze fell on the door behind her, his message clear.

Opal huffed and turned, mumbling under her breath as she saw herself out. She wondered how many write ups she would get for hexing the cold-blooded bastard.

With his reputation, she'd probably get a parade.

———

QUINN'S PHONE WAS *RINGING*. It never rang. No one ever had the audacity to call him directly. Maybe it was the wrong number. It rang a second time, and he peeked at the caller ID.

Oh. That's who had the audacity. He reluctantly picked up the phone and greeted his boss.

"Hello, Mr. Wormwood. What can I do for you?" He dusted off his best customer service voice, but it was mediocre at best.

"Something's going wrong with my recorder, Devane. I need you to look into it and fix it." The older man's voice was gruff, and Quinn could barely hear him over the background noise. "I don't know how, but someone hacked into my recording files and hit me with a hex from one of my actual nightmares. "

Oh. *Oh, no.*

"My office is currently full of pixies, and they *bite*, Devane. *Hard.*" He swore loudly, followed by a tiny squeal that quickly faded. Quinn almost felt bad for the pixie that had presumably been tossed across the room with the strength of an enraged ogre who subsisted on a diet of whey protein and the tears of interns.

"Yes, sir," Quinn said quickly. "I'll clear my schedule and send someone up to sort out your office immediately. There was a similar ticket from a customer yesterday, so I'll cross reference it with-"

"*Fix. It.*" Wormwood interrupted, gritting out the words through clenched teeth. "And don't tell *anyone* about this." He hung up before Quinn could reply.

Quinn leaned back in his chair with a sigh. If Opal saw that the tickets were reopened after she left, he would never live it down. He couldn't open a new ticket without the customers seeing it. They would call in to ask about it, and she would find out anyway.

"Son of a bitch," he grumbled, and then clicked 'reopen' on both.

———

"HAH!"

Opal's hand flew to her mouth, her head ducking below the edge of her cubicle, but her coworkers were already staring. It was worth it, though.

About an hour after she left Quinn's office, she got yet another call about a device being hacked. She escalated the ticket with a note that this was now the third report of a data breach. While creating that ticket, she was absolutely delighted to find that he had reopened both of the original tickets, which meant that she was *right* and he was a *stupid, condescending, self-righteous...*

Whatever. He was looking into them now, and that's all that mattered.

When her shift was over, she clocked out and headed for the elevators. Rather than heading to the ground floor, she did her best to hide her smug grin as she made her way back to Quinn's office.

His door was open, lofi music drifting from the ostentatious speakers behind him. Opal tapped her knuckles on the door lightly as she stepped in. "Hello, again," she chimed, but he either didn't hear her or blatantly ignored her. Either was certainly possible, so she tried again with a little more volume.

"Shit," he shouted, jumping in his seat. He blinked furiously at her, like he was coming out of a trance. "Where did you come from?"

"Um, upstairs? Sorry. Didn't mean to scare you," she said, stifling a laugh.

"You didn't *scare* me. I was just focused." He seemed to finally register who was standing in front of him, because his startled expression quickly fell into a frown. "What, uh... What do you need, Opal?"

"Well, I saw that you had reopened the-"

"Let me stop you," he interrupted her. She scoffed, too stunned by his brashness to properly react. "I reopened them because there was a similar report from upper management and I wanted to cross-reference the bug reports." He had already turned back to his screens when he muttered, "It had nothing to do with your *visit*."

"I... you... but..." Opal sputtered, the gremlin in her brain still ping ponging between witty remark and homicide. She took a deep, calming breath before she chose violence. If he wanted to be an asshole, she'd kill him with kindness.

"Great," she finally said, her words dripping with fake cheer. "I'm already off the clock, but I've got nothing else to do tonight." His gaze whipped in her direction at that, eyebrows disappearing beneath his messy hair.

Opal grabbed a chair from the other side of the room and dragged it, *loudly,* across the room, plopping down behind Quinn's desk with him. His horrified face was worth every second of unpaid labor. "Let's get to work," she chimed with a saccharine smile, pulling her notepad from her backpack and helping herself to the pen on his desk.

"You're not going away, are you?" he asked with a resigned sigh. Opal just smiled in response, flipping through her notebook until she found the page about Maria. Quinn rolled his eyes and took a deep breath. He held it so long that Opal was sure he was just showing off at that point. "Fine," he eventually grumbled after a particularly extensive internal battle. "Show me your notes."

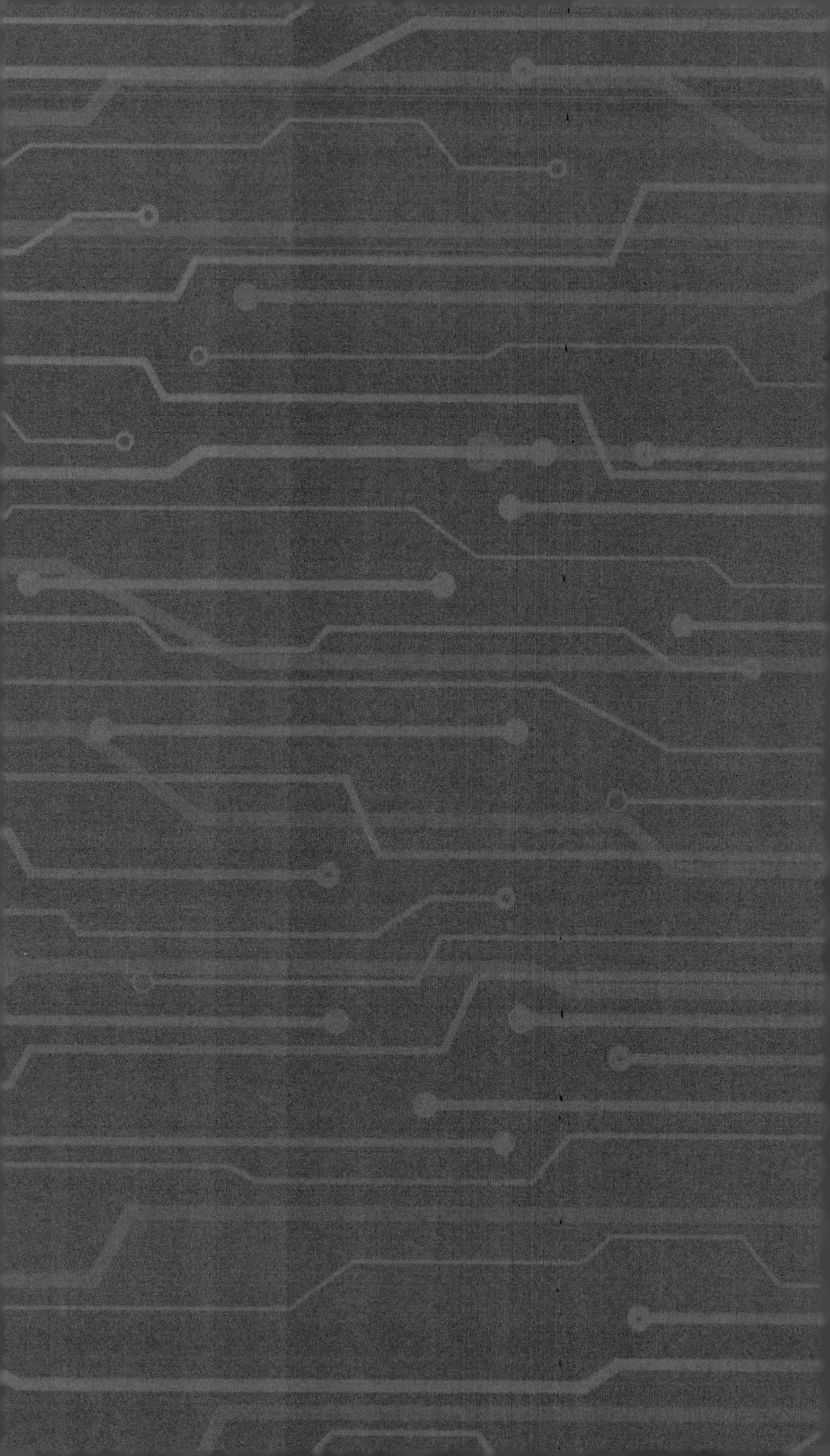

O nce they got into the groove of investigating, Opal noted that Quinn was much more agreeable. It was like he needed a warmup before he was able to be a decent person, which would be comical if it wasn't so frustrating. Their conversation didn't stray far from the task at hand, but it was professionally amicable.

Unfortunately, they had been digging for two hours and were no further in their investigation than they were at the beginning.

They cross-referenced the customers who reported issues, and the only connection they found was that all three of them lived on the same street. With Quinn's advanced clearance, he was able to look into the employee data, but there were no active employees who shared the street. Quinn suggested that the hacker may have been using a public access point, so they searched the area for any coffee shops or hang outs to no avail.

Opal employed every iota of self-control in her body to refrain from pointing out that he had finally admitted that there *was* a hacker.

The area was completely residential. *Barely,* Quinn had commented when they pulled up the satellite images. Opal pointed out that *she* lived in an identical neighborhood, and Quinn had the good sense to look ashamed. He had kept his comments to himself after that.

After hours of scrolling through the logs they pulled for each ticket, they determined that they showed no abnormal activity other than a singular breach and a quick download. They were all within 10 minutes of each other, and they all traced back to the same Dreamedia IP address.

Quinn's hopes that the last report would show a different origin were in vain, and he was forced to admit that the attacks were likely coming from inside the building. She was surprisingly graceful about it, but he suspected that it was because she was too tired to come up with a clever retort.

This discovery had prompted Quinn to tell Opal about Wormwood's report. At this point, it was relative to the case, so he figured the need to share outweighed the need to obey orders. After Wormwood's call earlier, Quinn had sent the cleaning staff up to his office to capture the pixies, but there was still the matter of where they came from.

"Well, there's no chance that *he* lives in the same neighborhood," Opal commented with a yawn, and Quinn nodded in agreement. It was nearly midnight, which was just about lunchtime for him but probably well past bedtime for her.

"No," he agreed. "Definitely not. So, that throws a big wrench in our location theory. It's still too much of a coincidence that the other three live in the same area, but there has to be a different factor connecting Wormwood."

"And you're sure there aren't any employees who live on that street? Or maybe nearby?" Quinn shot her a wry look in lieu of a response. "Right, okay," she conceded, holding her hands up in surrender. "Of course you are. Well, now what?"

Quinn chewed his lip while he considered the next logical step, and one long fang stuck out. Opal thought it was adorable until his stomach growled, and she was reminded that he was, in fact, a sanguivore.

There weren't many vampires in the city, but most of them were on a strict synthetic or animal diet. She'd heard about back rooms in private clubs throughout the city where one could find a more taboo food source, though. She knew he came from a rich and important family in the vampire community, but she wasn't sure what his proclivities were.

"Excuse me," he mumbled, standing from his chair, and Opal sucked in a breath. She let out a quiet sigh of relief when he bent down to grab a bottle of synthetic blood from the mini-fridge behind them, and was immediately embarrassed by her assumption. What did she think he was going to do? Lean over and bite her? *Stupid.*

"I think we need to talk to these customers in person," Quinn suggested. He leaned one elbow on the counter while his bottle spun around in the microwave. Opal opened her mouth to agree and was stopped by a yawn. "Tomorrow," he added. "I think we should wrap up for tonight. You're not going to be of any use to me if you're dead on your feet."

Opal wanted to argue with him, but he was right. Even if he was infuriatingly condescending about it.

"Okay. What time should we... Can you, um..." She stumbled over her words, trying to find the right way to ask without being offensive. Quinn quirked a patronizing eyebrow at her and she was reminded exactly who she was talking to. Decorum be damned. "Can you walk in the sun?" she blurted out.

He *laughed.*

"Yes, Opal. I can walk in the sun. It doesn't feel great, but I won't burst into flames. Holy water doesn't hurt me, either." The microwave beeped and he grabbed the bottle, sitting back down at his desk before turning back to her. "Sorry to disappoint."

Heat crept into her cheeks, but she wouldn't let him make her feel stupid. There were hundreds of different creature races in Stratos. She couldn't be expected to know everything about them all. "Great," she said, ignoring his comment. "How about ten? We can meet at Maria's house."

"Who's Maria?" Opal narrowed her eyes at him, not sure if he was messing with her or not. "Kidding," he laughed.

"I didn't know you knew how to do that," Opal said.

"Do what?"

"Laugh," she told him with a smirk. He rolled his eyes, but there was no malice in it.

Maybe he wasn't so bad.

Opal sat on the bench at the bus stop by Maria's house, tapping her foot impatiently. Quinn was ten minutes late. He hadn't bothered to text her, despite exchanging numbers before she left the night before.

She finally heard the rumbling from his motorcycle coming around the corner and hopped up to meet him. She considered making him wait out of spite, but she was eager to get going. He pulled up next to her as she walked up the short pathway from the street to Maria's porch and the engine faded to a dull roar before stopping completely. He pushed out the kickstand with one foot, but kept his full cover helmet on.

"Finally," Opal complained. "I thought you were ditching me." Quinn followed her onto the covered porch in silence before taking off his helmet. He stuck it under his arm, but his gaze was glued to the floor.

"Sorry," he muttered quietly. "I had to deal with a call, and... It doesn't matter. Sorry." He seemed to genuinely feel bad for making her wait, and she was horrible at holding grudges, anyway.

"Wow, Devane. That was two apologies in the same breath," she chided him with a grin. "I suppose that warrants forgiveness." The tension in his shoulders melted away and he finally looked at her, the corner of his mouth tipping up slightly. "You ready for this?"

"After you," he said, taking a step back and sweeping a gloved hand in front of him between her and the door.

Opal stepped up and knocked. A muffled reply came from somewhere inside the old brick house, followed by creaking footsteps coming down a flight of stairs. The door opened a few inches, stopped by a short chain, and a pallid woman with wild black hair peeked through the gap.

"Can I help you?" Her voice was strained, and she went into a coughing fit before either of them could reply. "Sorry, came down with something yesterday and none of my remedies are working."

"Sorry to hear that," Opal said, taking a discreet step backwards. "We won't take up much of your time. Are you Maria?" The woman nodded. "I'm Opal. We talked the other day about your dream recorder being hacked. And this is Quinn. He's the head of Cybersecurity at Dreamedia."

"Oh, hi! Why, uh… Why are you at my house?" Maria's gaze narrowed suspiciously over Opal's shoulder at Quinn. She *definitely* knew who he was. Or, at least, *what* he was.

"Well, we were looking into your report," Opal explained. "There have been a few similar calls since then, and we're trying to figure out where the connection is. Do you know if there's anyone who might want to target you specifically?"

"I mean, I run an all-purpose apothecary." Maria tipped her head toward the neon sign in her front window advertising fortunes, favors, and functional cures. "Not one of those phonies, either. I do good business. Not everyone is happy with their fortunes, though, and some people ask for too much and don't like to be told no."

"Could you give us the names of any recently disgruntled customers?" Quinn asked. She stared at him with distrust for a moment before answering.

"I keep a list of banned customers," she said slowly. "But I don't know if I should just hand it over. I don't want anything to happen to any of them."

"Nothing bad will happen to them," he replied with a tight smile. "Unless, of course, we discover that they're hacking into Dreamedia devices." The alarm on her face prompted him to add, "In which case, we would alert the police." She didn't look convinced.

"We just want to cross reference with the other customers," Opal assured her, taking over the conversation before Quinn lost his forced composure. "If I could just take a picture of your list, I promise to delete it when we're done."

Maria's gaze bounced silently between them for a moment before she backed up and closed the door entirely. Opal's shoulders sagged in defeat just as metal scraped together on the other side of the door. It swung open, fully this time, and Maria held out a scrap of paper covered in scribbled names.

"Take a picture, but you make sure nothing happens to them," she said quietly, glancing in Quinn's direction briefly. "Please let me know if you figure out who did it. I'm positive that this flu is magical, not viral. I'll need to find who hexed me so I can make a counterspell."

"You got it," Opal promised as she pulled out her phone and snapped a photo. "Thank you so much for your help. I hope you feel better soon!" Maria just nodded and shut the door.

When Opal turned back to Quinn, his polite smile had fallen into an annoyed scowl. "Sorry," she offered. "That was a bit much."

"It's fine. I'm used to it." Without warning, he slid his helmet over her violet hair, pressing a button on the side to lift the visor. She blinked at him, not sure what was happening but not wanting to interrupt him. "I'm sure she knows exactly who I am. My family isn't exactly well-liked among the working class here. They own most of the businesses in town, and they couldn't care less about the people who keep them rich."

"But not you?" Opal asked, carefully venturing into the dangerous territory of personal details.

"No," he said with finality. "Not me. Let's go." With that, he stepped off the porch and hopped on his bike, gesturing behind him with a nod.

Opal followed, the visor concealing any evidence of the heat rushing to her cheeks. It was surely from the helmet, she told herself, and not from the impending proximity and physical contact.

No, she would *not* be getting hot and bothered over Quinn Devane. He may not be terrible to look at, and have a *very* nice bike, and have at least enough social awareness to acknowledge his own privilege, and occasionally surprise her with something resembling gentlemanly etiquette, and... *Shit.*

With a deep breath, she swung one leg over the back of his bike and wrapped her arms tightly around his waist. For safety, of course. His fingers brushing the backs of hers lightly before taking off was accidental, obviously.

———

THE NEXT STOP WAS VALOG, the construction worker who was attacked by a glitter bomb in the form of a gigantic beam. He only lived a few blocks down from Maria, but Quinn's face was bright red by the time they pulled up to his house. Opal realized that the glass visor of the helmet probably had a UV light filter on it to protect his face. She pulled it off quickly and handed it back to him.

"I appreciate the concern, but I think you need this more than I do," she told him, but the redness was already fading now that they were in the shade of the orc's house.

"I'm fine. You're breakable," he told her. "I'll take this one." He brushed past her and knocked on the door. They waited a while, but no one answered. He was about to knock again when a giant man with deep green skin and tusks protruding from his bottom jaw came around the back of the house.

"Valog?" Quinn asked, stepping between Opal and the orc.

"That's me," he replied. "Who's asking?"

"Quinn," he said, nodding back at Opal. "And Opal. We're from Dreamedia. Looking into your report. Can we ask you a few questions?"

"Wow. I didn't think DM made house calls," he chuckled. "Come on in."

"Sorry 'bout the mess," Valog told them when they stepped inside. "Still can't get rid of it." Quinn looked around the sparkling room, his face a mask of abject horror. Opal was trying desperately not to laugh. There were splotches of glitter covering almost every surface in the room, from the couch cushions to the floor to the doorknobs.

"So," Opal started, since Quinn was still paralyzed in the doorway. "Can you think of anyone who might target you with an attack like this? An ex-girlfriend or something, maybe?"

"I don't think so. I don't really have any bad blood with anyone. I was thinking about it after we talked, though. My brother Zog lives here too, and he's… Well, he's kind of an asshole, if I'm being honest. He's got some buddies who come over and they get drunk in the yard and act like idiots. Some of them are a little sketchy, too. Maybe he pissed off a neighbor?"

"Maybe," Quinn said, finally joining the conversation. He didn't move from the doorway, though. "But, if that was the case, why wouldn't they go after your brother?"

"Well, they might have thought they were. We're twins."

"That's… unfortunate. Family can be a pain," Quinn said knowingly.

"Yeah, I love him, but he definitely causes some problems for me. And makes some questionable decisions."

"Do you think you could name off some of your neighbors that he may have had a bad interaction with? These are all rental properties, so we can't pull property records."

"Sure, but I have to warn you. It's gonna be a long one."

"The more, the merrier," Opal told him with a smile.

———

THE THIRD REPORT was from a werewolf named Emery, and she conveniently lived two houses down from Valog. The sun was blocked by clouds, so Quinn walked his bike down the sidewalk under the shady safety of the trees while Opal scanned the lists for any overlap. There were a handful of names on both lists, so she used a bit of illusion magic to highlight the duplicates on Valog's handwritten list.

They stopped in front of the house and found a woman digging in a little garden in the front yard. Quinn nodded to Opal before stepping into the shade, and she walked over to the woman. As she got closer, she noticed the woman had earbuds in. She reached down to tap her on the shoulder, but the woman turned and growled before Opal could even make contact.

"Sorry," she said quickly, jumping back with her hands in the air. The woman pulled out an earbud and stood to face her. "Didn't mean to startle you!"

"Oh, hon. No, I'm sorry. I've got a hair trigger sometimes. I assumed you were that asshole down the block." She brushed her dirt-covered hands on her old denim shorts before offering one to Opal with a warm grin. "I'm Emery. What can I do for you?"

"We spoke yesterday about your dream recorder," Opal

said, taking her hand and shaking it with a little squeeze. "You said you think it might have been hacked?"

"Oh, yeah! You must be Opal! Wow, a house call and everything! I must be special," she laughed. "Yeah, it was super weird. I had a dream the night before that I was being harassed by these phantoms, but they were just, like, mocking me? And then I woke up yesterday and my room was just full of them. Making fun of my hair and my clothes and whatever they could find. It's bizarre."

"That *is* bizarre," Opal agreed. "Are they still there?"

"No, they disappeared while I was at work yesterday."

"Oh, good. Well, we're investigating these claims, and we have a list of suspects from some other people who were attacked. I wanted to see if maybe you recognized any of these names? Or maybe add to the list?"

"We...?" Emery looked around, her gaze finally finding Quinn in the shadows of her front porch. "Oh," she muttered, the tiniest wrinkle forming between her brows. She turned back to Opal without another word, but her concern about a vampire hiding out next to her hydrangeas was clear.

Opal was starting to feel guilty about her opinions on the vampire. Yesterday, she assumed he was just a pompous, rich jerk. After seeing the way the average person treated him, his attitude toward the world was making a little more sense.

She held the paper out for Emery to inspect, and it didn't take long for her to point out a name.

"That one. Charles Dawson. If one of these people did it, it's him," she said with absolute certainty, pointing at a name in the middle of the page.

"You're sure?" Opal asked.

"Oh, definitely. I just moved here a few months ago, so I don't know many people. I don't even recognize most of these names, and the ones I do know are friends. But I just broke up with Charles last week and he did *not* take it well."

"Oh, no," Opal said. "I'm sorry to hear that! What happened, if you don't mind me asking?"

"Well, we hadn't been together for long. He was fun when we first started dating, but he just got really gloomy and wouldn't talk to me about whatever was bothering him. Then, I guess he lost his job and, when I offered to help him find a new one, he just snapped on me. I told him that was the last straw." Emery crossed her arms over her chest, as if reinforcing her conviction. "I wasn't going to waste my time dating someone who just dragged me down all the time."

"Good for you," Opal agreed, nodding her approval. "Okay, that's really helpful. Thank you!"

"Would you happen to know where Charles was working before he lost his job?" Quinn asked quietly.

"Um, well..." Emery started, eyeing him cautiously. "Sorry, I figured you already knew. I don't know exactly what he did, but he told me he worked with you guys. At Dreamedia. "

"Interesting..."

"I think we need to pay Charles a visit next," Opal suggested, glancing over at Quinn. He tipped his head in agreement. "Would you happen to know where we can find him?"

"I sure do," Emery told her, pointing over her shoulder. "That grey house with the rose bush by the steps. I've never actually been in it, but I know that's where he lives. We met when I was moving in, actually. He was sitting on his porch and saw me dragging boxes in, so he came over to help."

Opal met Quinn's gaze again, quiet anticipation in her eyes.

"Thank you so much for your help, Emery," Quinn said, lifting one leg over his bike. "We'll see what we can find out, and hopefully prevent any future attacks."

"Y-yeah," Emery stammered in return. "Thanks." She seemed to be weighing his words for sarcasm, but there was none to be found.

"Shall we?" Quinn held his helmet out to Opal, a smirk playing on his lips. She took it with a grin and hopped on the bike behind him like it was second nature. If she wasn't careful, she was going to make a habit out of this.

"We shall."

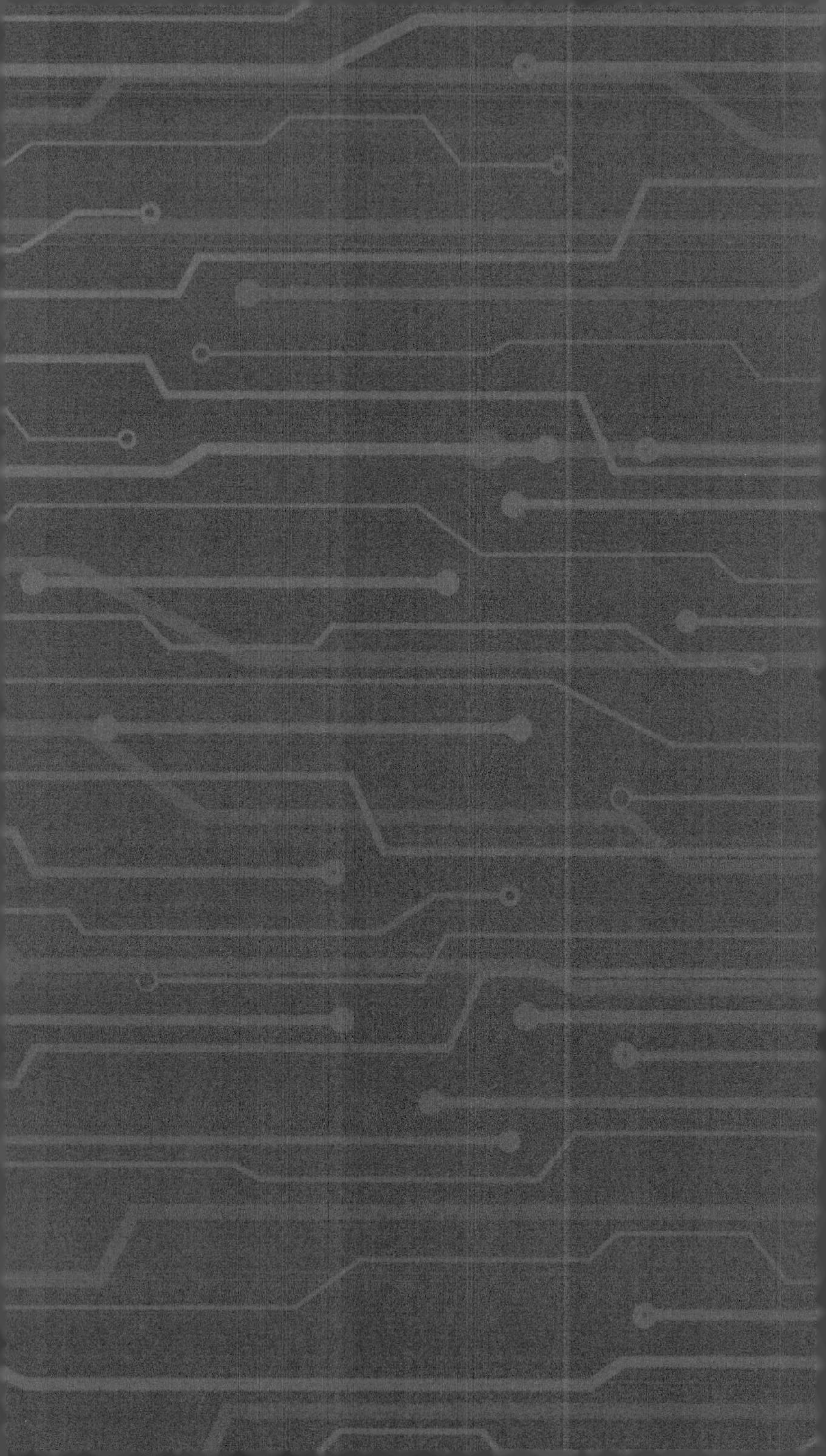

"Let me take the lead on this one," Quinn said as they walked up the porch steps. "Who knows what this guy is capable of."

"Okay," Opal agreed. "But I'm keeping the cops dialed and ready, just in case." He wanted to tell her that was an excessive precaution, but they had no idea what they were walking into, so he just nodded and rapped his knuckles on the weather-stained door.

It took a few long minutes after he knocked, but the door finally swung open to reveal...

A man.

Just a human man, and a sad excuse for one at that. He was short and thin, with dark, greasy hair hanging past his eyebrows and darker, greasier flannel pajamas full of holes. His eyes were rimmed with red, and his skin was waxy and pale.

"What," he mumbled, but it was barely a question.

"Are you Charles Dawson?" Quinn asked.

"Who's asking?" He hiccupped, and Opal was sure by the smell of it that the air in front of him was *definitely* over the legal limit.

"My name is Quinn Devane. We'd like to-"

The next few seconds were a blur of motion that Opal couldn't hope to keep up with. As soon as Quinn said his last name, Charles' eyes flew open. He stepped back, pushing the door shut. The door stopped short of closing as it slammed into Quinn's foot, and his hand shot out to push the door open again with preternatural strength.

"Not so fast, Charles," Quinn growled, stepping over the threshold as the man retreated through the living room. Opal followed them at a safe distance, more worried for the man than for Quinn now. He stalked through the only open pathway in the cluttered room toward what looked like the kitchen.

"I'm not going to hurt you, Charles," Quinn called out. "But you're going to tell me exactly how you broke through my firewalls." There was a symphony of clashing metal in the kitchen, and Quinn's face contorted into a feral grin. "There you are."

Opal blinked and he was gone, nothing but a flutter of dust on the floor where he had been standing. She ran to the doorway and found Quinn hunched over behind the kitchen table, a pair of slipper-clad feet kicking frantically beneath him. A pile of dirty metal pots and pans lay on the ground next to them, thrown from the sink when Charles tried to climb through the open window behind it.

"Quinn!" Opal cried out, and his head popped up from behind the table. "Are you okay?"

"Oh, I'm great," he told her. "Caught him trying to scramble out the window like a coward." He stood, hauling Charles up to his feet by the collar and plopping him down unceremoniously in one of the rickety chairs around the table.

Opal was ashamed to find herself searching his neck for bite marks. Even more so when she found none.

The man's eyes were heavy, barely open despite the chaos, and his head lolled from side to side. Quinn clapped his palm on Charles' cheek. Maybe a little harder than he needed to, in Opal's opinion.

"Alright, Charles. How did a drunk like you get past my security?" Quinn demanded, dragging two empty chairs between Charles and the door and sitting down. He leaned forward, elbows on his knees and fingers laced, and glanced purposefully between Opal and the second chair. She took a seat next to him.

"Hey!" Quinn shouted when Charles didn't respond. He flinched at the noise, suddenly bursting into tears. Quinn leaned back in his chair with a deep sigh as Opal leaned forward.

"Charles, can you tell us why you did this? What happened?" Opal's voice was soft and soothing, and Charles finally looked up at her with a sniff.

"I... I didn't... I don't know what you're talking about." He stumbled over his words, half of them slurred. "I didn't do anything."

"Oh, please," Quinn huffed, and Opal shot him a look.

"We have enough evidence to connect you to at least three of the attacks," Opal told him. "And we know you used to work for Dreamedia. We're not here to haul you off to jail. No one was actually hurt. We just want to know *why*."

"And *how*," Quinn added, quieter this time. Opal gave him a tiny nod of approval.

"No, I..." Charles started, and then groaned in defeat. "Okay, fine. Yes, it was me, but I had every right."

"Okay," Opal said, heading over to the counter. "Let's get some coffee and a blood clearing tonic in you and you can start from the top."

———

"I MOVED to Stratos a few years ago with my mom," Charles explained. His words and hands were both steady now, but he still looked like someone had stuck him in a microwave. "She, uh... She was pretty sick, and we lived in a little town a few hours from the city, so we moved here to be closer to her doctors. It's so much more expensive to live here, though, and her treatments weren't cheap either."

"I have an IT degree. I figured I would be able to find a good job in the city, but no one would hire me because I'm non-magical. At home, no one cared. Here, though, it's like a neon sign above my head that says I don't belong. I finally found a job..."

He hesitated, glancing at Quinn with contempt.

"At Dreamedia. They said there wasn't any room in the IT team at the time, but they would put me on the janitorial staff until a spot opened up. Six months tops, they said. Minimum wage for back-breaking physical labor. Money was tight already and only getting tighter, so I didn't have a choice. I agreed, thinking I could tough it out for six months."

"I'm guessing it wasn't six months?" Opal said with a sad smile.

"No, it was not. That was three years ago. Three years of being treated like shit or ignored completely. I don't even know which one I hated more, but I did it. I came in early, stayed late, and busted my ass to impress literally *anyone* who might be able to pull some strings for me. No one cared," he spat, shooting another glare at Quinn.

"I'm sorry, is this somehow *my* fault?" Quinn asked incredulously. "You keep looking at me like I kicked your puppy, but I've never seen you in my life."

"You're one of them!" Charles seemed to have surprised himself with his own outburst, following it up with a much quieter, "Never even gave me a chance."

"So, you did all of this because you didn't get a promotion?" Opal was trying to understand, but it seemed like quite the overreaction.

"No, they..." He leaned back in his chair with an exasperated sigh. "A few weeks ago, my mom took a turn for the worst. She had a congenital heart defect that was being stabilized by magic, but it has to be reapplied every month. It was starting to wear thin, and we set an appointment for after my next payday so we could get it renewed, but..."

His voice cracked, his mouth twisting up in an attempt to hold back the tears that were threatening to fall. Opal reached out and patted his forearm, and Quinn's gaze darted to the point of contact. He stared the man down, daring him to do anything untoward.

He did not. With a steadying breath, he continued.

"Anyway, she didn't make it. She passed away last week, and I wasn't even home to be with her because I was at my awful job. She died *alone*. I came home and... and I found her. I requested a few days off to deal with the funeral and everything, but my supervisor denied it because it wasn't requested in advance. As if I could have anticipated it? Not that I'll be able to afford a funeral anyway. I couldn't even force myself out of bed the next day, though, so I didn't make it in."

Opal pursed her lips, already knowing what happened next. She glanced over at Quinn, who clearly had no idea what was coming.

"Wormwood sent me an email that afternoon telling me I was fired. Couldn't even be bothered to call and check on me or ask why I didn't make it in. Three years of outstanding service down the drain over one missed shift."

"That's why you didn't show up in the employee address search," Opal mused. "You weren't an employee anymore." Charles nodded.

Quinn's brow crinkled, and he crumpled his jeans in his fist. None of this was sitting well with him.

"There had to be something else," he insisted. "Wormwood is a dick, but he can't fire you for *one offense.*"

"Oh, but he can," Charles assured him sardonically. "That's what it's like to be the lowest of the lower class around here. It was in my hiring contract that I could be let go for any reason at any time."

"Why... Why would you sign something like that? Didn't you have a lawyer look over it?" Opal's mouth fell open. She knew Quinn came from a wealthy family, but she didn't realize *how* wealthy, apparently.

"With what money?" Charles spat. "I signed it because I had no other choice. It was the only way to put food on the table. He lured me in with the promise of working directly for *you*, but that was never going to happen. It was just a carrot on a stick to fill the jobs that no one wants to do. That's the consequence of being born non-magical with generational debt instead of a silver spoon between your fangs."

He put as much venom in his words as he could, but a broken man could only bite so hard. Opal fully expected Quinn to bite back with another patronizing remark, but he shocked them both by holding both hands up in defeat.

"You're right. I apologize," he said quietly. Opal kept the 'three in one day' comment to herself with no small amount of self-control. "I have no idea what it's like to be in your shoes. If I had known Wormwood was using my department to..."

"Well, now you know," Charles interrupted. "Do something about it." His gaze dropped to the floor and he added, "Or don't. I don't even care anymore."

"I will," Quinn vowed, and Charles scoffed. "I mean it. I won't be used as a false promise. Now, I understand why you'd want to target Wormwood, but why the others?"

"The witch helps everyone, but she refused to help me. I offered to pay, and I would have come up with the money, but she wouldn't work with me at all."

"What did you ask her for?" Opal asked.

"A spell to fix it. Something to take me back in time, even just a few weeks. I could bet on the stock market or play the lottery or something, and then I could quit my job and be there for my mom before she… I might not have been able to save her, but I could at least make her last few weeks enjoyable."

"Oh, sweetie," Opal said. "She couldn't have done that even if she wanted to. We're legally and magically bound when it comes to time magic. If she tried, it would have backfired and she would have been arrested immediately."

"Oh," Charles breathed. "So it wasn't just me?"

"No, I bet it had nothing to do with you at all. We talked to Maria, and she was very nice. I have no doubt that she would have helped you if she could."

"Well, that orc definitely had it coming. He cornered me in the street on my way home from work a few weeks ago and mugged me. Stole my wallet and my house keys. I had to change the locks and replace all my cards, but I couldn't do anything about my cash. I reported it to the cops, but they said they couldn't do anything without evidence."

"He sounds like he deserved it, but you got the wrong guy on that one," Quinn told him. "The orc who mugged you was Zog, but you hacked his twin brother, Valog. And glitter-bombed his entire construction crew."

"Shit," Charles hissed.

"And my shoes," Quinn added, twisting his foot to show the thick layer of glitter still stuck to the bottom of his black sneakers.

Charles gave him a sheepish grin. "That was a good one," he said, and Quinn swiped the bottom of his shoe on Charles' filthy pant leg, leaving a sparkling smear below his knee. "Yeah, that's fair," he grumbled.

"And Emery?" Opal asked. "We know the two of you were dating and she broke up with you. I'm guessing you didn't tell her about all of this?" Charles dropped his gaze to the floor again.

"I didn't want her to know how pathetic my life is," he admitted. "I was shocked that she was interested in me at all, and I didn't want to ruin it by telling her I live with my sick mom and mop floors for a living. So, I just kept it all to myself."

"So, you kept the most important parts of your life a secret from your girlfriend, and when she got tired of you keeping her at arm's length..." Opal trailed off, not sure how to finish her thought in a nice way. It was a pretty stupid way to go about things, if she was being honest.

"Yeah, I've realized that part was entirely my fault. I used the counterhex that came with the phantoms as soon as I calmed down and thought it through." He was clearly ashamed, his watery eyes avoiding contact with either of them. "I should probably apologize."

"Yes, you probably should," Opal agreed. "But, I think

she'll understand if you just tell her the truth. The *whole* truth."

"Yeah, maybe." He looked up at her with a small, hopeful smile. "Thanks."

———

QUINN STILL HAD one burning question.

"So, I have to know. How exactly did you get past my firewalls? You did all this after you were already fired, so you wouldn't have had any access inside the building."

"Oh, I knew this was coming eventually. A few weeks before I was fired, I planted a bug in the server room that gave me remote access from up to about ten miles. It's connected to my laptop via a combination of tech and borrowed magic. I just had to get within range of the devices I needed to download data from and activate the bug to initiate the transfer of downloaded files."

Quinn looked like he was going to be sick. Opal didn't think it was possible for him to be any paler than normal, but his face was a nearly transparent shade of green.

"You… You bugged my server?!"

"Sorry. I'd say it's nothing personal, but…" Charles shrugged. Quinn's eye was twitching.

"You realize you'll need to remove that bug immediately,

right?" Quinn's eye was twitching. Opal was trying *very* hard not to laugh.

"I'll consider it," Charles said. "Fine, fine. I'll come remove it," he added when Quinn rumbled with a low growl.

"Where did you even get a bug like that?" Quinn demanded.

"I, uh... I designed it myself. I studied ethical hacking in college."

"That is definitely *not* ethical hacking," Quinn muttered.

"So, how did you pull off the magic part?" Opal asked. "Those hexes were pretty impressive, to be honest."

"I hired a gremlin to help with some of it, but most of the hexes were just spells that I bought from a shady artificer a few streets over. I sold some of mom's jewelry to pay for it. Once I downloaded their recent nightmares, it was just a matter of figuring out how to make them come to life."

Opal bobbed her head, impressed with the creativity.

"I didn't have any intention of hurting any of them. I just... I wanted them to feel a little bit of the suffering they caused me. It was stupid."

"No, I get it," Quinn assured him. "It's not stupid. I might not be able to understand your plight, but I can definitely see why you would want these people to pay. Your execution was good, but your alibi was a little... lacking."

"Thanks, I think?"

Suddenly, Quinn was struck with an excellent idea.

"Charles, how would you like to *actually* stick it to the man?"

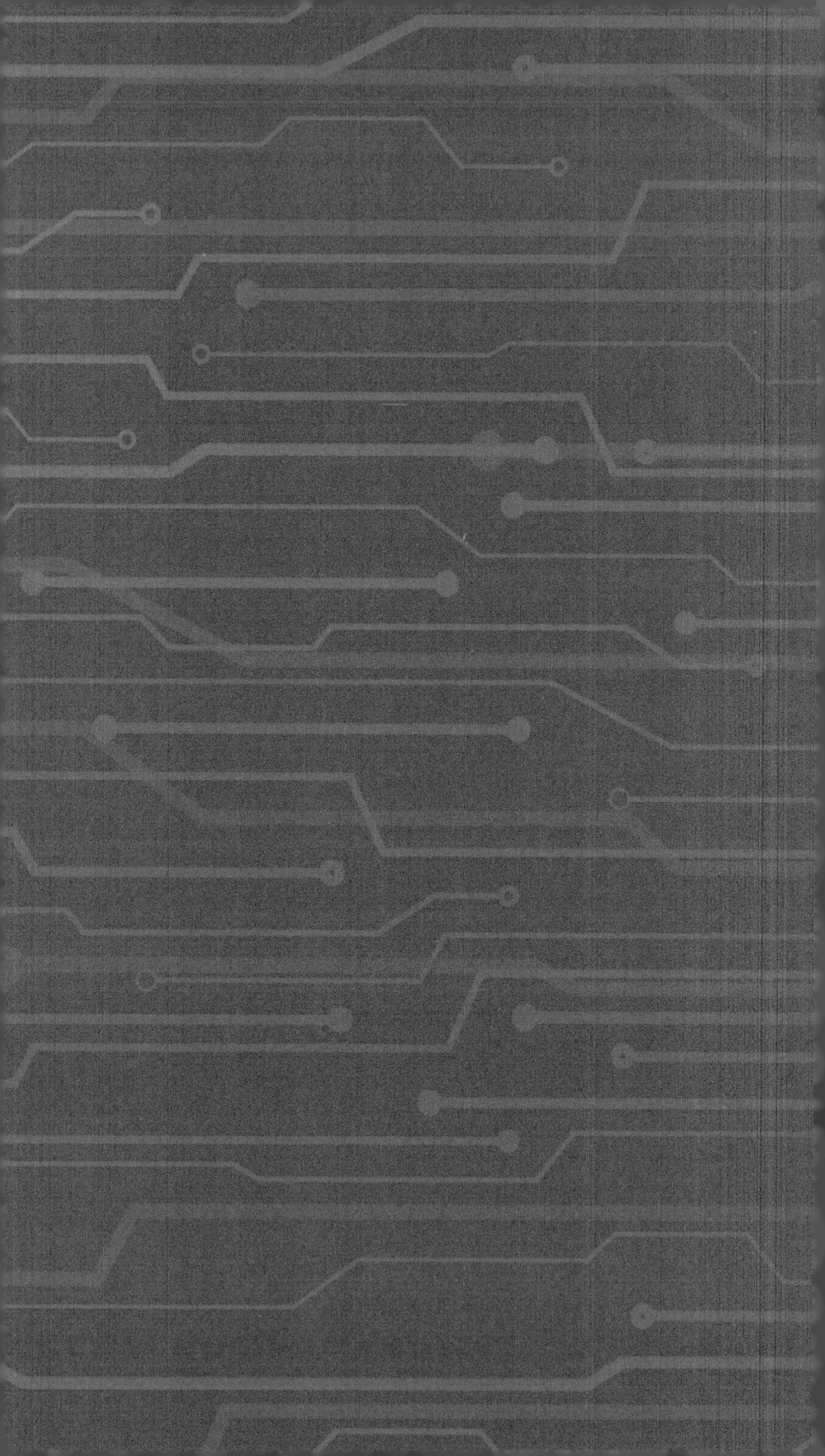

ONE WEEK LATER

"Welcome to the team, man. We're excited to have you." Quinn clapped Charles on the shoulder. He'd been a little nicer to everyone over the last week. His team had suggested a possible body snatcher situation.

The truth was that he finally had a little bit of freedom from his family, and he had every intention of using it to cause a little chaos at Dreamedia. His father had called him the morning of their investigation to let him know that the position in the family business that they had been holding for him had been filled, which roughly translated to 'we've given up hope that you'll become a respectable lawyer one day'.

At first, he was devastated. Not that he wanted the position, or the attention, or the constant proximity to his family, but the idea of them just giving up on him was a lot to deal with. After their interaction with Charles, though, he realized that there was a lot that he could do with his newfound freedom.

Since his family hadn't cut him off financially, he still had access to their excessive wealth. His first order of business was to help Charles pay for the funeral his mother deserved and get his bills up to date. Charles refused at first, but Opal convinced him.

"Let him spend his money on you," she had told him. "Consider it exposure therapy for his empathy." How could he argue with that?

Quinn had also informed the board of directors at Dreamedia that Wormwood had been forcing people into contracts with the promise of a promotion that would never come and firing them without cause. It turned out that they were *not* aware, and they were not happy at all about the reputation Wormwood was creating for their company amongst the working class.

He was fired that day.

Quinn also pulled some strings and opened up a new position in the IT department. Head of Ethical Hacking. When he informed the board that a human had helped them identify the source of the breach and neutralize the threat, they were more than happy to make some room in the budget for Charles.

They didn't need to know *all* the details.

Charles' first assignment, *after* removing the bug, was to make sure no one would ever be able to use a bug like it again. He was thrilled to get started.

Quinn and Opal met up with Charles on his lunch break, eager to hear about his first day.

"It's going great," he told them. "Everyone is so welcoming. It feels good to be doing something I care about, too. I can't thank you both enough." Opal gave him a warm smile.

"Just keep my security tight and we can call it even," Quinn told him.

"Deal."

Opal and Charles ate quickly, scarfing down the street tacos she bought from the food truck outside. Quinn watched, nose wrinkled in mild disgust, while he sipped a warm bottle of Pulse through a straw. When they were done, Charles thanked them for lunch and headed back to work.

"You're done at eight, right?" Quinn asked, lingering at the table. His fingers tapped anxiously on his thigh. He was trying to appear cool and nonchalant, but Opal saw right through it.

"I am," she said, mercifully deciding not to chide him for it.

"Would you, uh... Do you want to... Maybe..." He was floundering. Failing miserably. He practiced this for an hour last night. "Um, dinner or..."

Opal couldn't contain her laughter anymore, and Quinn frowned. "Right, nevermind." He planted a hand on the table to stand and leave before he embarrassed himself any further.

"No, sorry," she said quickly, laying her hand over his on the table. "I'm not laughing at you. Well, I am, but it's just... If someone told me a month ago that Quinn Devane would be asking me out, I would have had them committed. And here you are, beating me to the punch."

Quinn tilted his head at her, puzzled.

"I was going to invite you to my cousin's show tonight. His band is playing a few blocks from my house, and I thought you might like them."

"Oh," he said, all the tension flooding from his body. "Um, well... I wasn't really sure how we would do dinner anyway," he laughed. "That sounds nice. I'll wrap up early and I can drive us straight there after work."

"It's a date," she told him with a grin.

CLICK FOR CHAOS

LAYLA NOX

ACKNOWLEDGMENTS

Thank you to the team at Fables & Filth for organizing the Ink & Intrigue anthology and for hosting the Discord festival!

My wonderful beta readers, who jumped on this story as soon as I sent it because I worked on my draft until the last minute in true ADHD fashion.

My indie author friends who encouraged me to write something new and out of the norm for me. I had a great time, and I'm glad I stepped out of my comfort zone!

My momager, who has taken her role very seriously. I couldn't do this without you.

INK & INTRIGUE

This short story was written as part of the Ink & Intrigue anthology from Fables & Filth. You can find more information about Fables & Filth and get the entire anthology at:

https://www.fables-and-filth.com/

Join us on Discord!

https://discord.gg/3kG2Py2ACJ

ABOUT THE AUTHOR

Author portrait by @teoctobart

Layla Nox is an author of urban fantasy and dark romance from Ohio. She loves to explore worlds filled with magic and morally gray characters, drawing inspiration from her love for all things dark and spooky. When she's not writing, she can be found reading, playing video games, or working on a new craft project.

Instagram/Threads: @laylanoxauthor

TikTok: @laylanoxauthor

Facebook: Layla Nox (@laylanoxauthor)

ALSO BY LAYLA NOX

Mortals & Muses Series

Marginally Yours

Shattered Verse

Others

Click for Chaos

CLICK FOR CHAOS

LAYLA NOX